MW01141566

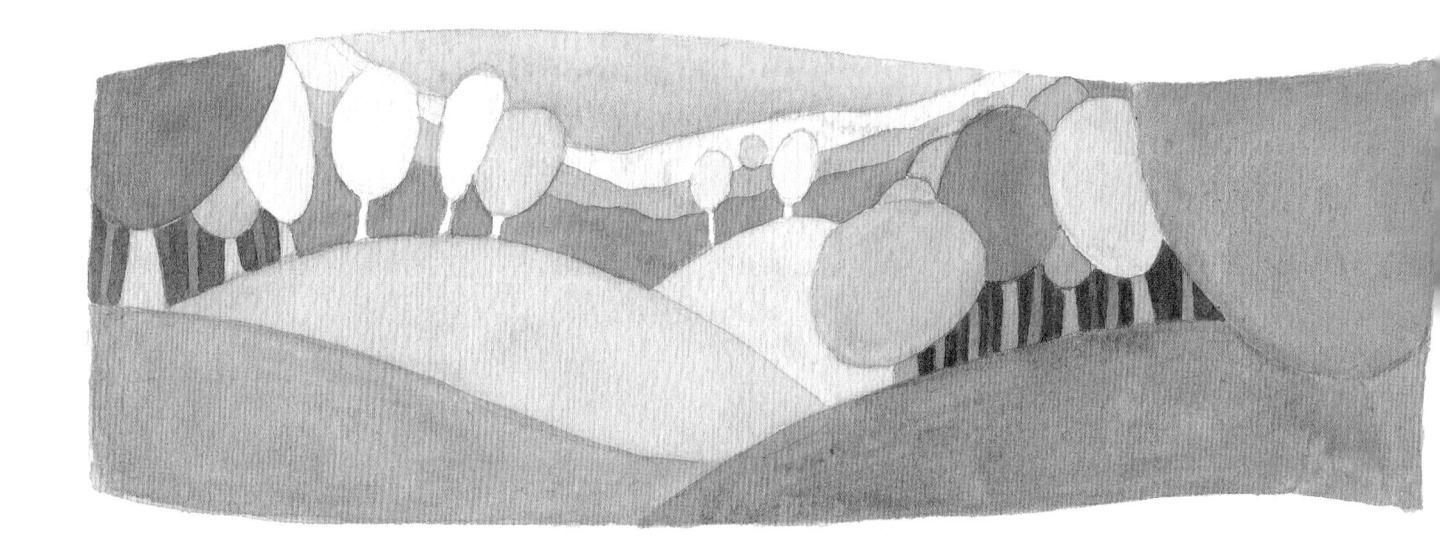

ABOUT THE STORY

When I was at Cornell, I was lucky to be able to study with Harold
Thompson, author of the acclaimed *Body, Boots, and Britches.* He
encouraged me, during the spring break, to travel to West Virginia.
There I knocked on cabin doors and at last collected three wonderful
African-American tales, including *Tailypo!* and *Little Eight John,*
which later won a Coretta Scott King award. Then, on a Fulbright
scholarship to Denmark, I studied folklore and folk literature.
From an 1836 farm newspaper I unearthed an early Hans Christian
Andersen tale, *The Woman with the Eggs,* which, adapted as a
picture book, became an ALA Notable. In England, a charwoman
at the Cromwell Hotel took me to meet her grandmother, whose
childhood favorite folktale was *Little Johnny Buttermilk.* It is a joy to
be able to retell this story; it has become a favorite of mine.

—JW

And Little Johnny Buttermilk
lived with his ma and pa
happily,
in a red house,
in the green country,
under a blue sky,
for the rest of their lives.

But when she untied the sack, only smashed bits of her best china fell out. This time, the old witch was so angry she really did burst.

She unlocked the door— rushing
in with a hammer. CRASHH!
"That's the end of you!" she cried.

By the time she came back,
Johnny was at the market
selling buttermilk.

He climbed up the
chimney to the roof

and

jumped

down.

After the door was locked, Johnny took out a knife, and cut a hole in the sack. He filled it with all her best china. He sewed up the hole.

She tumbled him into her sack and dragged it away. Almost home, she remembered, "I bought a hammer in town. I left it at the shop! I must go back."

She carried the sack to her house and put it on the floor. She locked the door.

"This time you won't get away," she said, and went to town.

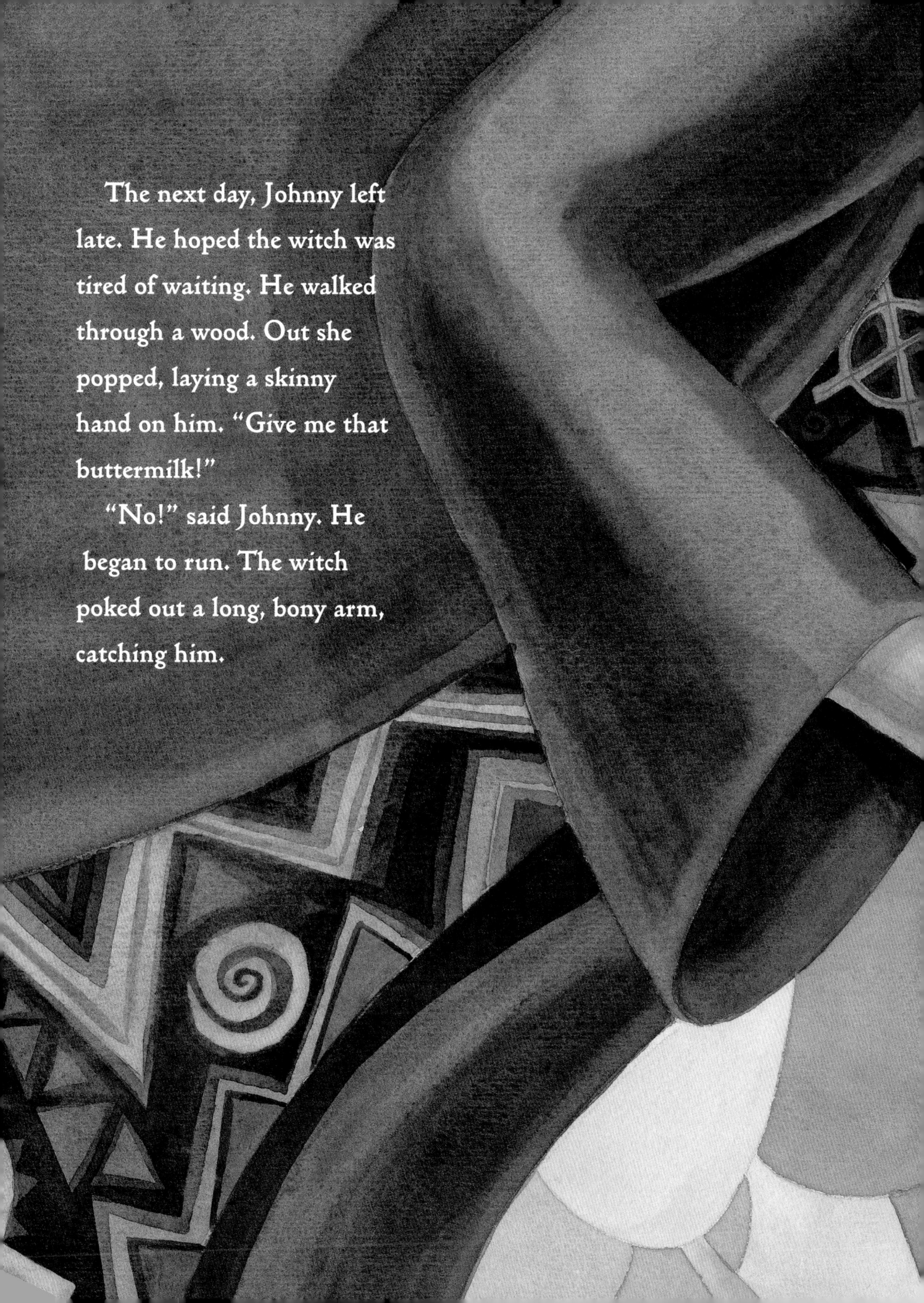

The next day, Johnny left late. He hoped the witch was tired of waiting. He walked through a wood. Out she popped, laying a skinny hand on him. "Give me that buttermilk!"

"No!" said Johnny. He began to run. The witch poked out a long, bony arm, catching him.

When the old witch came to pick up the sack, it was so heavy she could hardly carry it. It bumped all the way home until she was black and blue. "That boy got fat," she said, and untied the sack in the kitchen.

When large rocks fell on her toes, she almost burst in anger.

When she was gone, Johnny called, "Get me out of here. She wants to boil me in buttermilk!" He told them to fill the bag with large stones. And he thanked them and took another road to town.

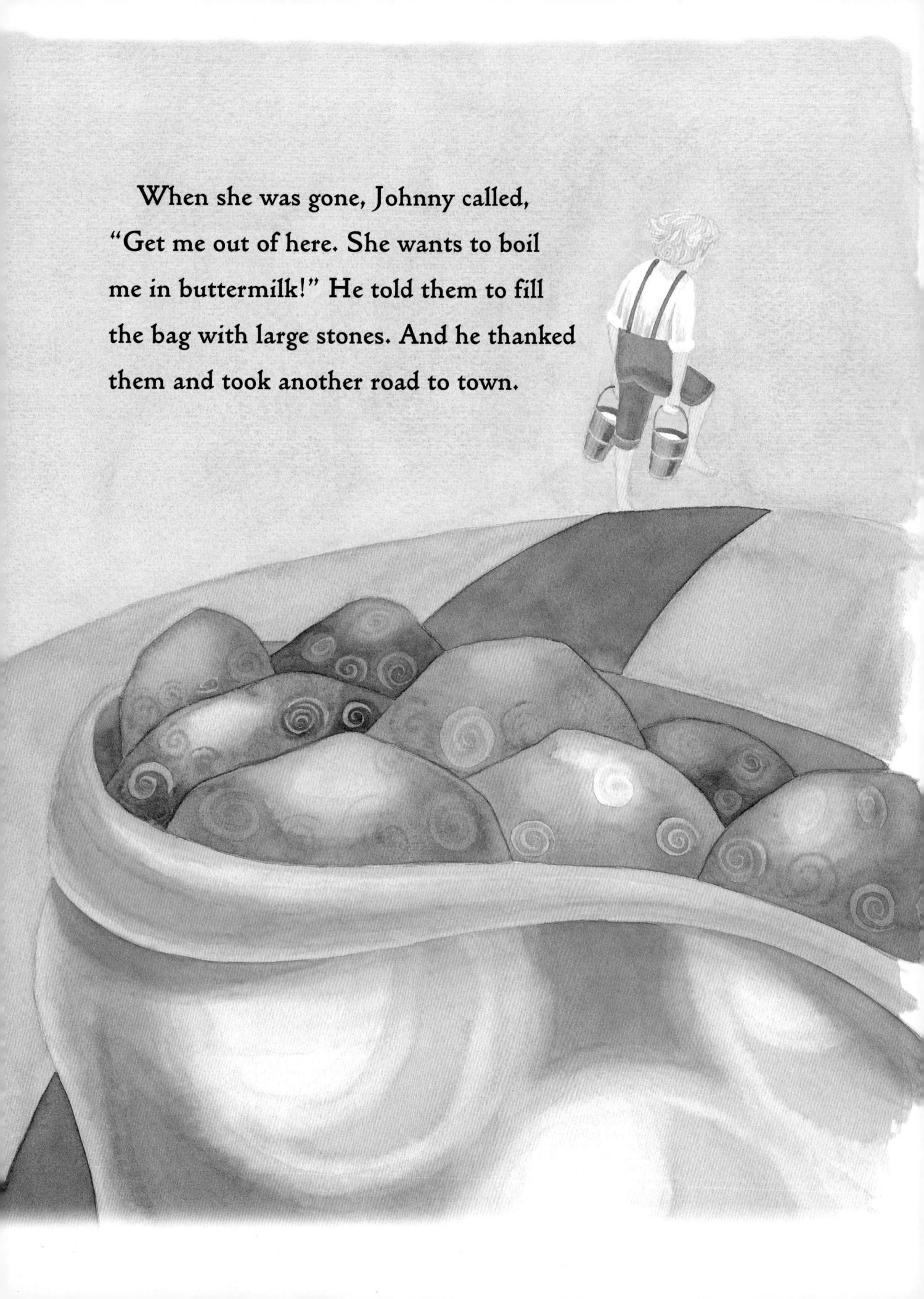

Suddenly—she remembered, "I bought a set of
plates in town! I forgot them. I must go back before
someone steals them."

She saw three men fixing the road. "Watch my
sack," she told them.

"Then I'll take you and BOIL you in it!" she
yelled. She threw him and the pails into her sack.

Next morning, Johnny went to town early with his
pails. She was waiting. "Give me your buttermilk!"
"No," said Johnny. "I must sell it."

Back came the witch holding her pot. She took the sack and swung it over her shoulder and went home.

"That boy has grown bristly," she said. When she untied the sack, thorns and thistles fell out.

When she was gone, Johnny called, "Let me out. That old witch will stew me!"

He told the men to fill the sack with thistles and thorns. He thanked them and took another road to town.

Halfway home, she remembered, "I bought a pot
in town and left it at the market stall. I must go back
before someone steals it."

Two men were cutting a hedge. "Watch my sack,"
she cried, and she hurried to town.

Near Johnny's pa's farm lived an old witch.

One day, she met Johnny with his pails of buttermilk.

"Oh," whined the old witch. "Give me your buttermilk!"

"No," said Johnny. "I must take it to town to sell it. I can't give it away."

"OK," yelled the witch. "I'll TAKE it— and you, too. I'll stew you for supper!"

Every day, he walked to town with pails of buttermilk.

Every evening, he returned with empty pails and pockets full of coins.

He was called Johnny Buttermilk.

He saw his pa feed the hogs.

"Can I help you?" he asked.

"No. Wait till you are older," said his pa.

Then he saw his ma make butter.

"Can I help you?" he asked.

"Well," she said, "you can take the buttermilk to town each day, to sell it. My legs are tired. Yours are young."

There lived
under a blue sky,
in the green country,
in a red house,
a boy named Johnny.

to Amanda Lee Casselton

from Uncle Mouse

-J.W.

to my teachers and my students

-J.M.

Text © 1999 by Jan Wahl.
Illustrations © 1999 by Jennifer Mazzucco.

All rights reserved. This book, or parts thereof, may not be reproduced in any form without permission.

Published 1999 by August House LittleFolk, P.O. Box 3223, Little Rock, Arkansas 72203

501.372.5450

http://www.augusthouse.com

Book design by Mina Greenstein

Printed in Korea

10 9 8 7 6 5 4 3 2 1

Library of Congress Cataloging-in-Publication Data
Wahl, Jan.
Little Johnny Buttermilk : after an old English folktale / Jan Wahl ; illustrated by Jennifer Mazzucco.
p. cm.
Summary: Little Johnny Buttermilk must escape from the witch who keeps trying to steal his pails of milk,
until finally he outwits her once and for all.
ISBN 0-87483-559-3 (alk. paper)
[1. Folklore—England.] I. Mazzucco, Jennifer, 1972- ill. II. Title.
PZ8.1.W126Lj 1999 398.2'0942'01—dc21
[E] 99-13121 CIP

The paper used in this publication meets the minimum requirements of
the American National Standard for Information Sciences—Permanence of Paper for
Printed Library Materials, ANSI.48-1984

Little Johnny Buttermilk

after an old English Folktale

Jan Wahl

illustrated by Jennifer Mazzucco

AUGUST HOUSE
LittleFolk